Regina Calhoun Eats Dog Food

Other Avon Camelot Books by
Lynn Cullen

THE BACKYARD GHOST
MEETING THE MAKE-OUT KING
READY, SET—REGINA!

LYNN CULLEN grew up in Fort Wayne, Indiana. She received a bachelor's degree from Indiana University and did postgraduate work in education at Mercer University and Georgia State University. She lives in Atlanta, Georgia, with her husband and three daughters.

Regina Calhoun Eats Dog Food

LYNN CULLEN

AN AVON CAMELOT BOOK

VISIT OUR WEBSITE AT
http://AvonBooks.com

For Michael

REGINA CALHOUN EATS DOG FOOD is an original publication of Avon Books. This work has never before appeared in book form.

AVON BOOKS
A division of
The Hearst Corporation
1350 Avenue of the Americas
New York, New York 10019

Copyright © 1997 by Lynn Cullen
Published by arrangement with the author
Library of Congress Catalog Card Number: 96-96906
ISBN: 0-380-78803-9
RL: 4.9

First Avon Camelot Printing: February 1997

CAMELOT TRADEMARK REG. U.S. PAT. OFF. AND IN OTHER COUNTRIES, MARCA REGISTRADA, HECHO EN U.S.A.

Printed in the U.S.A.

OPM   10   9   8   7   6   5   4   3   2   1

1

The Third Wheel

Regina Calhoun slung one arm around Margaret, the other around Kate. She was just where she preferred to be—in the middle.

"I'm going to count to three," Regina explained as other kids scuttled past, trying to beat the morning tardy bell. "When you hear 'three,' " she said, "stick out your right foot, like this."

She took an exaggerated step forward, making the skirt of her Queen of Angels School uniform flare. Someone had left open the main entrance, letting in a balmy May breeze. Regina loved May. It was her birthday month.

Margaret lunged forward, following Regina's example. "I think I've got it," she said, her eyes round with seriousness behind her wirerim glasses.

Kate stared at the ceiling as if counting the dots in the tiles. "Can we just do it? The bell's going to ring."

Regina shivered with excitement. Already she could hear the laughs they were going to get.

"Ready, set—go!"

She plowed forward.

A solid weight at the end of her arm dragged her to a halt.

Kate hadn't budged.

"Why didn't you move?" Regina cried.

Kate broke free, brushing Regina's dark tangled bird's nest of hair with her elbow. "You said to go at the count of three," Kate said calmly. "You never counted."

"You knew what I meant," Regina said, glancing at Margaret for support. "Ready, set, go, is the same as one, two, three!"

"Not to me," said Kate.

Regina gaped in outrage.

"It doesn't matter," Margaret said quickly. "The bell's going to ring. If we don't get started now, we won't get to do our funny walk at all."

Kate pushed between Regina and Margaret. "All right," she said, draping her arms over their shoulders, "right foot first. One, two—three!"

Before Regina could protest, she was striding forward at the end of Kate's arm.

Robbie Colberg, skinny and pale as a cooked noodle, and two other boys poured in through the front door.

"Siamese triplets, coming through!" Kate exclaimed.

The boys laughed. Robbie Colberg guffawed. Margaret giggled so hard her palomino ponytail shook.

2

Regina fumed. The silly walk had been her idea. She should have started it. She should have been in the middle. She should have been the one raking in the laughs. Instead she was lumping along on the outside, as unimportant as a third wheel, and her birthday was in four days! It wasn't fair.

They marched silly-style past the door of the school office. Out of habit, Regina checked for the principal, Ms. Yoder. Since the evening of the talent show, during which she had danced and lit firecrackers (only little ones! that didn't even go off!) being around Ms. Yoder made her uncomfortable. The veins on Ms. Yoder's neck had throbbed so during their conversation that night.

Ms. Yoder was not in the office.

Regina looked over her shoulder as they marched on. Strange—Mrs. Greenway, the school secretary, was gone, too. No one was in the office. No one at all.

Regina's gaze landed on something on Mrs. Greenway's desk. The microphone for the P.A. system.

Regina pulled out of Kate's grip. Excitement pumped through her body as she ran to the office. Now she was going to get what she was born for—the big laughs. She'd give herself an early birthday present!

"Regina?" Margaret called after her. "Regina, where are you going?"

"Oh, let her go," said Kate.

Inside the office, Regina snatched up the microphone. She scanned the names of the classrooms posted on the switchboard. Roberts, DeWitt, Montello . . . *Amsden*. Regina flipped a switch and blew into the microphone. "Hello?"

A male voice cackled over the speaker. "Yes?"

Regina lit up. Mr. Amsden! "Give me a cheeseburger, a Coke, and a Giant Fry to go."

Background laughter sputtered over the speaker. "Regina?" Mr. Amsden said, sounding tired now. "Is that you?"

"Oh, and I'll take a chocolate sundae. With nuts."

There was more distant laughter, followed by a heavy sigh. "All right, Regina, drive around."

Hugging herself with joy, Regina ran back into the hall where Margaret and Kate were waiting for her.

"I can't believe you did that, Regina," said Kate. "Amsden's going to kill you."

Regina stopped, stunned. "No he's not. He thought it was funny."

Margaret sighed, her gray eyes sad. "Oh, Regina, don't you ever *worry?*"

Regina didn't have to worry. Margaret did enough of that for both of them. "Not really."

"Well, maybe you should worry sometimes," said Kate. "You're always overdoing it." She gave Regina a slight smile. "I'm only telling you this for your own good."

Her own good? Regina swished her tongue over her chipped front tooth. Telling somebody something that wasn't nice could never be for their own good. Kate was just jealous that Margaret and Regina had been best friends first.

4

The bell rang.

"Oh, no!" cried Margaret. She bent into a run.

Kate jogged to catch up, then ran backward. "Regina, aren't you coming?"

"Yes—when I'm ready." Regina made herself walk slow. She wasn't worried. She didn't have a worry in the world.

Did she?

2

Cut the Clapping

A round of applause thundered from the back of the room as Regina slipped into the classroom. Matthew Rogers was beating together hands as huge and thick as catcher's mitts.

Regina fought off the impulse to do a curtsy. Matthew might love her, but she didn't want him to think she loved him back . . . yet.

Mr. Amsden looked up from his perch on the corner of his desk, where he had been calling the attendance list. "Cut the clapping, Matthew. Regina, you're tardy."

Regina grinned. "It took me awhile to drive around."

Mr. Amsden gave her a pointed look. "Then you can eat your Giant Fries at recess—inside . . . *alone*."

Regina tried to keep smiling but her heart wilted like a month-old balloon. Hadn't Mr. Amsden enjoy her joke? Making her miss recess—

6

he might as well have told her to go on living, but to do it without food and water.

Mr. Amsden finished the roll call and hopped off his desk, the top of which came up to his thick waist. Several of the kids in the class were as tall as he was. Matthew was two feet taller.

"Gang," said Mr. Amsden, "next week, I'd like to try something special."

"Ya hoo!" Matthew shouted from the back of the class.

Regina hoped that Mr. Amsden would order Matthew indoors for recess, too. It might be fun to be worshipped one-on-one for a half hour. However, Mr. Amsden just said, "Try to keep a lid on it, would you, Matthew? Now, as I was saying—"

Regina's mind raced ahead. What could be special about next week besides her birthday? "Are you going to show videos all day?" she asked.

"No, Regina."

"Laser discs?"

"No."

"Old film strips?"

Mr. Amsden drew in a breath as if restraining himself. "We're having Career Week."

Regina gaped at Margaret. Though Margaret put her finger to her lips in warning, Regina blurted, "Career Week? That's special?"

"Do you think you could remember to raise your hand, Regina?" Mr. Amsden asked wearily. "Or would you like to eat your Giant Fries inside during recess for *two* days?"

Regina slumped down so far in her seat that

her bird's nest rested against the back of her chair. It wasn't fair. Her birthday should be in the middle of Circus Week. Or Recess-All-Day Week. Or just plain Regina Rules Week.

"To kick off Career Week," said Mr. Amsden, rolling a piece of chalk between his stubby hands, "Teresa Corvi's father has agreed to speak to us about his job as a veterinarian."

Regina scowled at Teresa Corvi, who smiled and tapped her cheek with a pencil engraved TE-RESA in gold. It seemed like everything Teresa owned had a golden TERESA on it. Regina's things were labeled with masking tape and faded marker.

"Dr. Corvi will be here this afternoon right after lunch," said Mr. Amsden, his chalk clicking against the blue stone ring that he wore on his right hand. It wasn't a wedding ring—Regina had asked on the first day of school.

Matthew shot up his hand. "What about recess?"

"We're having it this morning," said Mr. Amsden. "Tonight," he continued, "I want you to think about asking your parents to drop by our class to talk about their careers. I can schedule them for sometime next week."

Arley Campbell shot up his hand. "My mom's a dermatologist. That's a skin doctor. She can come if she's not in surgery."

"Great," said Mr. Amsden. "Have her call me at the school office."

Regina coolly studied Arley. Until recently, she had loved him with all her heart. But now, with his perfect dimples and perfect straight blond hair and perfect doctor mom, she couldn't stand

8

him. Especially since he had dropped her last month.

Margaret raised her hand. "My mother's a nurse who delivers babies. I think she'd come."

"That would be interesting," said Mr. Amsden, clicking his chalk. "Ask her to call."

Regina's mother answered the phone for Dr. Price, a pediatrician. Regina was thinking about asking her mother to come when Kate raised her hand listlessly. "I suppose," Kate said, heaving a sigh, "my mom will come, too."

A buzz rose over the class. Kate didn't need to say what her mother did. Everyone knew. Liz Glendenning was on Channel Four every night at six and ten.

"You think she'd really come?" asked Robbie Colberg, white spit gathering in the corners of his mouth as it did whenever he spoke. Regina called him Mad Dog. At recess, he liked to chase Regina and pretend to bite her. "I want Liz Glendenning's autograph!" he said.

"Me, too!" chimed several others.

Regina rolled her eyes. Liz Glendenning was just a mom who drove around in a dinky red convertible blaring old peoples' music—the Eagles—when she wasn't yammering on her cellular phone. Regina had been in her car once before, with Kate. It was no big deal.

From the back of the class, a voice boomed, "I think she's really nice."

Regina craned around in her chair. Had *Matthew* said that?

"She's always helping people," Matthew continued, "like on her special reports and stuff."

"Remember the show where she took all the homeless kids to the zoo?" Robbie said, spit flying.

"Or when she helped rebuild that house for the family that got hit by the tornado?" said Arley.

"Or," said Teresa, "took that horse into the hospital for a girl that was dying? I wished I were dying!"

I wish you were, too, Regina thought grumpily as she turned back around. Her eyes connected with the wooden crucifix hanging next to the door. *Just kidding.* She sank so low in her chair that her knees stuck out the front.

"Regina," said Kate, "your underwear is showing."

"Those are my P.E. shorts," Regina sniffed, though she sat up and put her legs together. She glanced again at the crucifix. Okay, it was her underwear, but somewhere in the world kids probably took P.E. in their undies. They ran around naked in the jungle, didn't they?

"I just thought you'd want to know," said Kate, adding in a whisper, "since you're part of the Awesome Threesome."

Regina frowned at the Smiley Face someone had carved into her desk. It was just like Kate to use the name "The Awesome Threesome" as if she had made it up herself. As a matter of fact, Regina had been the one to come up with the title when Margaret, Kate, and she had decided to become best friends the day after the talent show.

"So far," Mr. Amsden said to the class, "you've just mentioned mothers that could come talk with us. Dads are welcome, too, you know."

Regina tugged at her growing-out bangs. She wished she could ask her dad. He was the smartest, funniest, handsomest dad in the world—she looked just like him, too—but after Mrs. Glendenning came, who would want to hear him? Janitors, even smart, handsome, funny ones like Dad, weren't exactly exciting.

Later, when recess time came, Regina sat with her arms folded, watching the rest of her class file out the door.

"Sorry," Margaret mouthed from her place in line.

"Yeah, sorry," said Kate. "We'll take care of Stink Breath for you."

Matthew reached over Robbie Colberg and Teresa Corvi and gave Kate a rabbit punch on the shoulder. Kate squealed.

"Knock it off," Mr. Amsden warned.

Regina looked away, her tongue seeking her chipped front tooth the way other people sought their teddy bears or blankies. 'Stink Breath' was the nickname *she* called Matthew. Matthew should be punching *her*.

"I'll leave on the lights," Mr. Amsden told her as the last of the line shuffled out the door. "I'm going to walk the class out to the blacktop, then I'll be back. Ms. Sparks is waiting for us."

Regina put her head on her desk. As the sound

of footsteps receded down the hall, she imagined herself as an abandoned orphan, rags hanging from her body and a soiled kerchief tied under her chin. She nibbled on her pencil, pretending it was a turnip or cabbage or one of those other foods orphan girls ate.

She noticed a flash of red outside the window. Out on the blacktop, in the bright May sunshine, Matthew was dribbling a red bounce ball around Kate.

Regina dropped her pencil. Most recesses, Matthew circled around *her*.

Outside, Kate tried to snatch the ball out of Matthew's hands. Failing to get it, she latched onto Matthew's arm and hung like an eighty pound weight.

That was exactly what Regina would have done!

Kate wasn't happy just stealing Regina's cleverest lines. Now she wanted to take Regina's loudest fan—four days before Regina's birthday.

Regina latched her tongue onto her chipped tooth. She had to do something about Kate, fast.

3

~

Matthew's Diaper?

"Let's do our silly walk," Kate said, slinging her arms around Margaret and Regina as the class scuffed their way to the lunchroom later that morning.

Regina ducked from under Kate's reach. "Amsden will be mad."

Kate reared back in disbelief. "You care?"

"Maybe we'd better not, Kate," said Margaret, "not now. But maybe we could work on the silly walk tonight."

"Tonight?" said Regina.

Margaret looked puzzled. "Aren't you coming?"

"Where?"

Margaret shot Kate an uncomfortable look. "Kate's."

"Kate's?" Now it was Regina's turn to be confused.

Kate clapped her hand over her mouth. "Oops!

I forgot to ask you!" She gave Regina a guilty smile. "Can you come over after school?"

Regina blanketed her tooth with her tongue. Sure Kate forgot. Well, she wasn't going to let Kate steal away Margaret that easily. Not four days before her birthday. "I'll call my mom at work after lunch."

"Oh," said Kate. "Good."

Just then Matthew thudded up on his size ten-and-a-half adult black gym shoes. "Ar-ley's got some-thing for Mar-gret," he sang.

The girls looked over to where Arley stood in the lunch line. He hung his head.

Though with her birthday coming, it seemed more fair that Regina be the one getting the present, Regina mustered a smile. Margaret deserved an admirer, even though it was that creep, Arley. "Way to go, Margaret. Maybe it's a ring or something."

"Oh, no," said Margaret. "It wouldn't be a ring. I don't think I could take one, anyway."

"If you're worrying about me, don't," said Regina generously. "I wouldn't like Arley now if he crossed the lunchroom on his knees for me."

"You did that for Mr. Amsden," Kate pointed out.

"I only circled his table," Regina corrected.

Margaret opened her lunch bag. "It's not you, Regina. I don't think my mother would let me take jewelry from a boy. When you take expensive gifts that means you're serious."

"Oh."

"What's he giving her?" Kate asked Matthew.

14

"That's for me to know and you to find out," Matthew called, his shoes thumping as he skipped toward Arley in line.

"You and Arley sit with us at lunch," Regina yelled after him. "Unless you're afraid I'll out-drink you again!" It was a great source of pride that when challenged last Tuesday, Regina had drunk nine containers of milk to Matthew's eight.

"You buy them, I'll drink them!" Matthew called back. It had been Matthew's contention that he'd only stopped at eight milks because he'd run out of money.

"Good luck!" Regina yelled, half-rising. She turned to Kate and Margaret. "You have any extra money? I want to buy fifty milks!"

"No," said Margaret. "I'm broke."

"There you go, Regina," said Kate, "overdoing it again." She snickered. "Anyway, Margaret spent all her money on Froot Loops."

Margaret glanced at Regina, struggling not to smile.

Regina dropped into her chair. "You bought *cereal?*"

Margaret shook her head *no*.

"Then what're Froot Loops?"

Kate burst out laughing. "Can't tell!"

Regina opened her lunch bag, scowling. Now they had their own in-joke.

What if the joke was on her?

Regina drew an apple out of her bag. Though her appetite had just died, eating sometimes helped when her stomach hurt. She had her apple positioned to the side of her mouth, away

15

from her chipped tooth and ready to bite, when Matthew bounded up.

"Want us to sit here?" he asked, pointing with his tray. The small paper bag that was sitting on top of his tray fell over on its side. Arley plodded up behind him.

"We don't care!" Regina exclaimed before Kate and Margaret could answer. She took a crunching bite of apple.

Margaret glanced at Arley, then wrung her ponytail.

"Only one milk?" Regina asked Matthew when he sat across from her. "Wimp!"

"You've only got one milk," he pointed out.

As Regina scoured her brain for a clever reply, Kate said, "Hey Arley, what'd you get Margaret?"

Arley froze in the act of sitting across from Margaret. He crouched like a coil ready to spring, his face as red as the Jell-O on his tray.

Regina could feel her lip curling. What was the matter with him? When he had liked Regina, he'd done all the things a decent boyfriend should do—insulted her, rabbit punched her, stole stuff from her until she screamed. But lately, for no reason, he'd become a blushing lump. Who wanted him?

Next to Regina, Margaret's cheeks turned the color of red bounce balls.

"Where's Margaret's present, Arley?" Kate persisted.

Arley glanced at Margaret, then hung his head. "In my desk."

Matthew shook the small paper sack that had

been sitting on his lunch tray. "Guess what I've got in here."

"Your dentures," said Kate.

Regina could top that. "Your diaper!"

"Your cat's hairball," said Kate.

"Your dog's booger!" shouted Regina.

"Good guesses," Matthew said, "but those aren't it."

"What is it, then?" Regina exclaimed, inflamed both by the competition and by talk of surprises near her birthday.

"Something for the woman I love."

"You, too?" said Arley. He glanced at Margaret, then dug into his Jell-O.

"Yep," said Matthew.

Regina gasped. She looked at Kate, only to find Kate looking at her. They turned to Matthew.

"Who's the woman?" they demanded.

"Can't tell," said Matthew.

Both girls sprang forward and pounded on his arms. "Tell us, tell us, tell us!"

"Nope."

Regina stopped pounding and sat back down. She knew why *she* was slugging Matthew—the surprise might be for her. But why was *Kate* so hot on the present . . . unless Kate thought the present was for herself.

She narrowed her eyes at Kate, who was still thumping Matthew. "Why do you want to know?"

"Can't tell." Kate stopped pounding. Matthew rubbed his arm.

Margaret looked away, smiling.

Regina sucked in her breath. It was true! Kate liked Matthew, and Margaret was in on it.

Robbie Colberg tottered over to the table with his Robot Boy lunch box. "Hey Regina, guess what I'm going to have for lunch?" he asked, spit flying.

"What?" Regina snapped. Across the table, Matthew was shaking his paper bag at Kate.

"YOU!" cried Robbie. He lunged forward, gnashing his teeth.

Regina held up her elbow. "Go away."

Robbie sagged. "Aren't you going to call me Mad Dog?"

"No."

"Oh." Robbie slouched over to an empty table.

Matthew laughed. "Remember when he chased you around the parking lot with that big booger on his cheek? He thought you were running from him because he was pretending to be a vampire."

Regina watched Robbie settle into his place and spread out a Thermos bottle, some plastic containers, and his collection of miniature robots.

"Yuk," said Kate. "I wouldn't touch one of his stupid robots for a million bucks. They probably have spit all over them."

Regina frowned at her lunch. "Robbie's not so bad," she muttered.

"Robbie?" exclaimed Kate.

Regina looked up. Kate, Margaret, Matthew, and Arley were staring at her. Finally, the attention she deserved. She sat straighter. "In fact, Robbie's kind of cute."

"Cute?" cried Matthew.

Regina sniffed. "Cuter than some boys I know."

"Robbie?" said Kate.

"Colberg?" said Matthew.

"Yes," she said, looking pointedly at Matthew. "He's nice, too. And funny."

"Funny?" said Matthew in a crushed tone.

"Are we talking about the same Robbie Colberg?" asked Kate.

"Yep." Regina ran her tongue over her tooth. Dare she push it? "Guess what? I love him!"

"You DO?" said Matthew, his voice cracking.

"Mad Dog?" said Kate.

Regina grinned. *Direct hit!*

Margaret groaned softly. "Oh, Regina."

4

Small Victories

That afternoon, Regina raced for the main door the moment the dismissal bell rang.

"Slow down!" yelled Kate.

Regina sped up.

Mr. Amsden stepped into the hall. "Regina—no running!"

Regina slowed to a brisk waddle. She reached the front door and turned around, gratified to see that she had made it before anyone else in the school. Today she would settle for even small victories.

"Do you see my mom?" asked Kate, sauntering up with Margaret.

"I wasn't looking for her," Regina said with a sniff. Not everybody was excited by Liz Glendenning. "I'm looking for . . ." She remembered her wild claim at lunch. ". . . Robbie Colberg."

"He's back in the room, gathering up his robots," Kate said. She peered through the glass doors as kids pushed outside, letting in blasts of warm air. "She's not here," she muttered to herself.

"Here comes Arley," Regina told Margaret. "Let's grab him and make him tell us what he got you."

"No!" said Margaret, horrified. "Look, there's Matthew. Why don't you make him give you *his* present?"

Hadn't it occurred to Margaret that Regina might not be "the woman he loved"? "I don't want his gross present," said Regina. "I'm in love with Robbie, remember?"

Margaret sighed, a worried look on her face. "I remember."

Matthew thundered up on his size ten-and-a-half gym shoes. "Hey Margaret, don't you want your present from Arley?"

Arley bolted forward and thumped him on the arm. "Shut up, Rogers!"

"Why don't *you* give away your present, Matthew?" said Margaret, her ears red.

Matthew pulled the little paper sack out of his backpack and shook it. "You mean my cookie?"

"Is that what it is?" cried Regina. She lurched forward, then stopped herself. She loved Robbie now. But if Kate loved Matthew so much, why was she just staring out the window? If Regina were her, she'd be wrestling the bag out of Matthew's hands this very moment.

"Nobody wants your dumb cookie," Regina muttered.

"Good," said Matthew, pushing open the door and galloping out to the curb. "Because it's for my mother!"

"His mother?" said Margaret.

"She's the only one who likes you anyhow!" Regina shouted as he got in the Campbell's car with Arley.

Matthew rolled down the car window and laughed wildly, not the effect Regina had hoped for.

Just then Robbie galloped up, a row of robots braced against his chest with his arm.

"Hey Robbie," Regina yelled, "you want to go out with me?"

Out in Arley's car, Matthew's jaw dropped. Kate turned around from the door.

Robbie blinked, then croaked, "My mother's waiting for me!" He galloped, pigeon-toed, to his car.

Matthew hung out the window, gaping, as Dr. Campbell drove out of the parking lot.

Twenty minutes later, Ms. Sparks, the P.E. teacher, rounded up the few kids still waiting for rides home. "Let's go," Ms. Sparks said, brushing off the sleeve of her white polo shirt. "Time to head to the cafeteria for Afterschool Care."

"My mom is coming," said Kate. "Can't we just wait?"

"Kate, you and I have been through this enough times for you to know the rules."

Kate's brow crumpled. Just then, a small red convertible zipped up the hill to the parking lot.

When it streaked to the curb, Kate plunked herself in the front seat.

"Sorry I'm late, girls," Liz Glendenning said as Regina and Margaret climbed in back. "We were filming a special piece and time just got away from me."

Kate clicked her tongue.

"What was the special piece about?" Margaret asked, leaning forward.

"The baby gorilla born at Zoo Atlanta last week."

"Awww," said Margaret. "Was he cute?"

Regina kept her face straight forward, but her gaze migrated toward Mrs. Glendenning.

"He was adorable," said Mrs. Glendenning, turning back to the steering wheel. "Actually," she said, driving away from the curb, "it's a little girl gorilla. I just wanted to kiss her wrinkly infant face!"

"Did you get to hold her?" Margaret shouted, the wind from the open convertible whipping her palomino ponytail.

"Oh, no." Mrs. Glendenning checked for traffic before darting her car out onto the street. "The mother hasn't let her out of her arms," she called over her shoulder. "She holds onto her baby twenty-four hours a day."

Kate clicked her tongue. "Gorillas make better mothers than some humans."

"Kate," Margaret said, her ears turning pink.

Regina saw Mrs. Glendenning's frown in the rearview mirror.

Regina ignored them all. She loved the way the wind felt in her hair, though she would have preferred that it stream behind her like Margaret's, instead of bobbing up and down on her head like a paddleball.

Kate folded her arms over her chest. "I suppose you're too busy to come to Career Week at my school next week," she said to her mother.

"Career Week?" asked Mrs. Glendenning. "What's that about?"

Kate glared at the CD player.

Margaret bit her lip. "Um, Mr. Amsden wants us to ask our parents to come talk to our class about their jobs," she said. "They're supposed to come next week, Mrs. Glendenning," —she glanced at Kate—"if they can."

Mrs. Glendenning glanced at Kate. "Do you want me to come?"

Kate shrugged.

"How about me coming tomorrow morning?" her mother asked.

"You're supposed to come next week," said Kate. "Tomorrow's just Friday."

Mrs. Glendenning didn't seem to hear. "Let me call Oliver to make sure he didn't schedule anything around ten for me." She picked up her car phone and punched in some numbers. "In fact, I wonder if I could get some of the camera crew to come with me. Hello—Oliver?"

"That would be so cool!" Margaret breathed as Mrs. Glendenning talked into the phone. "Do you think our class could be on TV?"

Kate scowled. "She was supposed to come next week, not tomorrow."

Regina sank back in her leather seat. If Mrs. Glendenning had to come to school, let it be tomorrow. There could be only one star next week—The Birthday Girl, Regina!

5

The House of Glendenning

Regina trudged, head down, through the entrance hall of Kate's townhouse. She was not going to gape at the photographs on the wall. Who cared about pictures of Mrs. Glendenning arm-in-arm with Big Bird . . . Elton John . . . the President of the United States? Regina had once met Happy the Clown with her Girl Scout troop.

The sounds of a piano being played drifted in from the next room. Regina pattered across the polished wood floor and peered around the corner. Margaret was seated at a huge, shiny grand piano, looking very small in her plaid school jumper. Her skinny legs dangled down from the bench as she picked out a song she had once told Regina was called "Au Clair de la Lune."

"This piano makes music sound so good," Margaret said to Mrs. Glendenning, who was standing behind her.

Mrs. Glendenning patted Margaret on the shoulder. "Come over and play it anytime."

Kate frowned at her mother, arms locked against her chest. "Somebody ought to play the dumb thing," she muttered. "No one else around here does."

"There's plenty of food out in the kitchen," said Mrs. Glendenning, slipping off her high-heeled shoes. "I just bought four kinds of Bob and Barry's ice cream, and there are frozen pizzas if you want them."

Regina's traitorous stomach gurgled in response. Since Dad had lost his job at Desk Pro and had taken the job as janitor at Northlake Mall, the only snack around her house had been peanut butter and crackers.

Mrs. Glendenning disappeared upstairs as the girls clattered out to the kitchen to eat.

A short time later, they filed with their bowls into a room that had as many books on its walls as the Queen of Angels School library. Kate plopped into a fat leather chair and blipped on the TV with a remote control. Regina tried not to gape, but the TV had a screen that was bigger than two refrigerators. She perched next to Margaret on a huge tapestry-covered couch.

"What do you want to do?" asked Kate, swinging her legs over the arm of the chair.

Regina pulled her attention away from the base of the coffee table—were those real moose antlers?—and turned her mind to more important things. "You know what? My birthday's in four days."

"We should practice our silly walk," Margaret said, jumping to her feet. "I'm not very good at it."

"I'll show you," said Kate.

"No! I'll show you!" Regina plunked down her bowl of ice cream. She'd hint about her birthday later. She wasn't letting Kate steal Margaret that easily. "Here, Margaret!"

They stumbled across the room, tripping over each other's feet. "I've got a better idea," Regina said after Margaret accidentally stepped on her toe for the fifth time. "Let's do the cancan!" She kicked up a leg. When Margaret tried to do the same, she fell straight onto her bottom.

"Such klutzes," said Kate, nonchalantly stirring her ice cream as they lay chuckling on the floor.

The phone rang.

Kate picked it up. "Hello?"

"I don't know, Regina," said Margaret. "Maybe we ought to figure out a silly *crawl*."

"Make that a silly *sit!*"

"Shhhh!" Kate hissed. *"It's Matthew."*

Regina sat up, suddenly serious. "Matthew?"

"He's says he's got another cookie," said Kate. "He says—"

"I don't care what he says!" Regina bellowed. First Arley had gone ga-ga over Margaret. Now Matthew was calling Kate. Soon the four of them would be hanging around together at recess . . .

at lunch . . . at P.E. Regina would be as left out of the action as a spare tire!

Mrs. Glendenning rushed into the room, buttoning a turquoise silk blouse with one hand, carrying black heels in the other. "Kate, get off the phone."

Kate glared at her mother.

"Kate, get *off* the phone."

"Gotta go, Matthew," Kate mumbled.

"Oliver just called on my business line," Mrs. Glendenning said as Kate put down the receiver. "Something has come up at the airport—a plane crashed."

Margaret gasped. "Oh, how horrible!"

"I'm covering the story. Sorry, girls, but I've got to take Kate to her sitter's. I may be gone all night."

Kate's mouth drooped, then hardened into a short line. "You can't come to my school tomorrow, can you?"

Mrs. Glendenning slipped on her shoes. "Surely we'll wrap this story before then."

"Yeah, right."

"Mr. Amsden's got me down for ten-thirty—I'll be there, Kate. Right now, though, girls, we have to move it. The Channel Four van will be pulling up any minute. Take your ice cream with you— you can leave the bowls in the truck."

Regina and Margaret scrambled off the floor. "This is so exciting!" Margaret whispered.

Regina pressed her tongue against her tooth. She couldn't top stories about plane crashes and baby gorillas. She couldn't produce rides in the

Channel Four van. She couldn't even attract Matthew Rogers. Compared to Kate, Regina was as boring as boiled rice.

Regina swished her tongue over her tooth. Well, she wasn't going to lose Margaret now. Not four days before her birthday. Somehow she was going to remind Margaret—and everyone else—how thrillingly exciting Regina Calhoun really was.

Even if she had to do something *insane*.

6

A Strangled Scream

Several hours after the Channel Four van had dropped her off at home, Regina strayed out to the kitchen, still wearing her school jumper. Neither Mom nor Dad had come home from work, and she was starved. She opened the cupboard. Her gaze landed on a box of Froot Loops.

Froot Loops, Margaret and Kate's in-joke.

Regina pushed the box behind a huge jar of pickles and grabbed an unopened box of Nutty Nuggets. She liked Nutty Nuggets better, anyhow. Much better. Besides, according to the picture on the back of the box, there was a big beautiful squirt gun inside.

She had just ripped open the box—wrong side up, but who cared?—when her sisters stormed down the hall.

Regina hid the box behind her back. Maybe one of her sisters had already claimed the squirt gun.

As the youngest in the family, Regina knew by long experience anything worth having had usually been claimed by her sisters first.

"Admit it, Maureen!" shouted Lydia. "You took my brush to school and you lost it!"

"I told you," snarled Maureen, who at fifteen was a year older than Lydia, but also several inches shorter. "I don't have it. Why would I want your filthy brush?"

"Because you always take my stuff. Whenever you lose or ruin your things, you come steal mine."

True, Regina thought. Where Lydia went wrong was keeping her stuff nice and in its place. Slobs can't resist stuff like that. Regina placed the box on the table. Her sisters had one minute to claim the squirt gun.

Maureen sniffed. "How would I ruin a brush?"

"With your nasty, bushy hair? Don't make me laugh!"

Regina's hand drifted to her own hair. Maureen's dark, thick but straight hair was a curtain of velvet compared to Regina's wiry bird's nest.

"If I were a beanpole like you," Maureen told Lydia, "I wouldn't go around insulting people's hair."

Tears swam in Lydia's eyes. "You are so mean! You try to turn all your friends against me, too. I wish we didn't go to the same school!"

"Oh, go cry like usual," said Maureen, digging through the refrigerator for milk. Regina glanced at the Nutty Nuggets box.

"If I want to, I will!" Lydia exclaimed. She

reached into the cupboard above the refrigerator where Mom hid cookies and drew out a box of Twinkies.

Time! The squirt gun was Regina's. She plunged her arm into the Nutty Nuggets, causing cereal to boil up around her elbow and spill down the sides of the box. Her fingertips connected with paper. She yanked out a package hardly bigger than a sugar packet. She frowned. This package was too little for the big squirt gun pictured on the box. Maybe this was just part of the squirt gun. The other parts were still inside the box. Before digging for the missing pieces, she tore open the packet. A two-inch plastic squirt gun dropped to the floor.

Lydia ripped the cellophane wrap from around her Twinkie. She narrowed her eyes at Regina. "You have my brush, don't you?"

Regina looked up from where she crouched over the squirt gun. It was the sorriest, puniest, most insulting excuse for a toy she had ever seen. "What?"

"Give it to me."

"You want it?" Regina held the squirt gun between thumb and forefinger as if it were a dead bug.

Lydia clicked her tongue. "Don't play dumb, Regina. Give me my brush. I can't get ready to go over to Samantha's house until I have it." She took an angry bite out of her Twinkie.

The brush. Regina'd been hoping they'd get over that.

She slipped the squirt gun in the pocket of her

jumper, thinking. At last she said, "I never brushed my hair with it." That was the truth, too. Still, she was glad there were no crucifixes in the room.

Maureen snorted. "Why don't you just blame Bones?"

Regina's mouth dropped slightly ajar. How did Maureen guess? As a matter of fact, Bones, the family yellow Labrador retriever, did have it. Though Teresa's smug face during Dr. Corvi's talk at school that afternoon had made it almost impossible for Regina to listen, something Dr. Corvi had said had sunk in. *A dog should be brushed every day.*

So Regina had brushed Bones. Right after she came home from Kate's. With the only brush she'd been able to find. Lydia's.

"Where is it, Regina?" Lydia demanded.

"Last I saw your brush," Regina offered, "was by the air-conditioning vent in the den."

Lydia wrinkled her nose in disgust. "Eeuuww, that's where Bones lays. That brush had better not stink!" She marched towards the den, cramming the last of the Twinkie into her mouth.

Dad jogged into the kitchen, wearing his gray janitor's uniform. "How are my gorgeous girls this evening?"

A strangled scream—the kind made by someone who'd received a shock while swallowing a full mouth of food—came from the den.

Dad's face creased in a lopsided grin. "Fine as usual, I see."

34

Lydia stomped back into the kitchen. "There are *dog hairs* in my brush! Re-gee-NA!"

Dad peered at the brush. "Let's see."

Lydia dangled the offending instrument from her fingers. A tuft of short golden hair drifted to the floor.

"H'mmm," Dad said.

"I'm not going to use this brush!" Lydia exclaimed. "Regina has to buy me a new one."

"I was only trying to do the right thing!" Regina cried. "Dr. Corvi said we were supposed to brush our dogs every day, so I did, the minute I got home. That was the only brush I could find."

"So now Bones is beautiful, and I'm a mess," Lydia snapped.

"Can't blame Regina for that," said Maureen, sipping her milk.

"Maureen," Dad scolded. "Regina, you didn't have to brush Bones that second."

Maureen drained her glass and put it in the sink. "Haven't you ever noticed? Regina always overdoes things."

"I do not!" Regina cried, her tongue flicking against her tooth as an uneasy feeling crept into her stomach. Kate had told her the same thing.

"Cool down, girls," said Dad. "Lydia, I'll get you a new brush. I have to go to Drug World anyhow to get some shaving cream."

Lydia brightened. "Now?"

"Sure."

Regina sighed with relief. Drug World was Lydia's heaven on earth. She never came home without a new kind of shampoo or nail polish or some other essential for her existence.

"And as for you—" said Dad, turning to Regina. Regina froze.

"—I'm going to hold you to your interest in Bones's care. Now that you made that brush officially his, I want you to brush him with it every day, just as Dr. Corvi said."

"Okay!" Regina agreed. "Bones likes it."

"That's not all," said Dad. "I've been working such long hours lately, Bones has had to wait longer than he should for his dinner. So I'm putting you in charge, Regina. I want you to feed him, day and night."

Maureen groaned. "Now poor Bones will never eat."

"You want to feed him?" said Dad.

Maureen stepped backward, shaking her head.

"All right, then. I'd rather Regina did it anyhow. It's time she took responsibility for something around here."

"I can do it!" Regina exclaimed. "I'll feed him right now! Here, Bones! Come on, boy!"

Bones pranced after her to the cupboard, waggling the back half of his body in joyful anticipation as Regina got down a large can of Dog E Dine.

"Let's go, Lydia." Dad opened the kitchen door. "Feed him twice a day, Regina. Two measures of dry dog chow in the morning, canned food in the evening—one can only. The canned food is mainly a treat."

"No problem," said Regina, waving the Dog E

Dine over Bones's head. Now his entire body wiggled. She cranked open the can, then tapped it over his dish. A speckled brown cylinder slid into the bowl with a moist *plop*. The mound was devoured before Lydia slammed the kitchen door.

The phone rang.

Regina answered. It was Margaret.

"Regina, turn on your TV!"

Regina cocked her head to listen for the sounds coming from the den. "It's on. Maureen must be watching it."

"Make her turn it to Channel Four. Go! I'll wait for you."

Regina put the receiver on the counter and walked toward the den. She stopped in the doorway as if nailed to the floor. A somber Liz Glendenning filled the television screen.

"Plane wreck," said Maureen, looking up from the couch.

"I know," Regina replied.

Maureen pointed toward the TV. "That's your friend's mom."

"I know."

"She is really cool."

Regina turned stiffly and marched back to the phone.

"Margaret?"

"Did you recognize that outfit? She was wearing it when she was with us. I can't wait until she comes to our school tomorrow. We'll all be celebrities!"

Regina swallowed. Margaret used to think Regina was pretty special. Not, evidentally, anymore.

"Gotta go, Margaret." Regina hung up the phone. She slumped against the counter, hardly feeling the steady *thump* against her leg. Bones peered into her eyes, hope radiating from his homely yellow face.

Regina sighed. "Am I cool, Bones?"

He whacked her harder with his tail. He couldn't have shouted "yes" any clearer in English.

Right then and there, Regina resolved that she would be the best dogkeeper in the entire world. Forget to feed him? Ha! She'd feed him *twice* as much—*three* times as much. She got out a can of Dog E Dine and slid another smelly lump into his bowl.

Bones wolfed down the food, then, seeing no more forthcoming, licked the bowl clean.

Regina wrinkled her nose. The only bad part about being the world's best dogkeeper was that she'd have to smell Dog E Dine every night. How could Bones stand the stuff? It smelled like a solid loaf of dog breath. Even the dry food she was to feed him mornings didn't stink as much.

Suddenly, it was as clear as the blue stone in Mr. Amsden's ring. Regina had the answer to being ignored by Margaret! No matter who Kate Glendenning's mother was.

Regina raced to the cupboard above the refrigerator.

7
∽

Precious Cargo

The following morning, as Maureen backed the ancient penny-colored station wagon down the driveway, Regina steadied the small paper bag perched in her lap. She looked up and found Lydia staring at her, her lip curled.

"Why don't you ever put your jumper in the wash?" Lydia said, stroking her hair with her new brush. "It is filthy."

Regina wanted to chuckle. If only Lydia knew what Regina had in her bag. She'd leap screaming out the other side of the car! There were grosser things in life than unwashed jumpers.

"Look twice before you back into the street," Dad instructed Maureen from the passenger's seat. It was the first time Maureen had driven to school since getting her learner's permit.

"I know, Dad." Maureen looked both ways twice. She blasted the Rust Bucket into the street.

"Too much gas!" Dad yelled.

Maureen stomped on the brake. Everyone rocked forward.

Lydia clicked her tongue. "You made me mess up my hair!"

Regina peered in her bag, fearful of her own disaster. She sighed with relief. Her precious cargo was intact.

She turned her mind to another important matter. "Dad?"

Dad turned his head, but kept his eyes on the road. "Yes, Regina?"

"Since I'm getting more responsible and taking care of Bones, do you think I could have a party on my birthday?"

"It's three days before your birthday," said Lydia. "You don't have time."

"Regina, we've already been over this," said Dad, his gaze still on the street. "Until I get my feet on the ground, we can't afford any parties. We can't even afford much in the way of presents. Your present is being able to stay in Queen of Angels school for the rest of the year. Your tuition isn't free, you know."

Regina frowned at the back of his seat. She couldn't help it that he lost his job at Desk Pro and had to work now as a janitor at Northlake Mall. At least she didn't have to change schools.

Maureen pulled the car to the curb.

"Why are you stopping here?" asked Regina. "Queen of Angels is two blocks away."

"I can't park when there are cars around."

"Oh, that'll be real convenient in a parking lot," Lydia commented.

"Go ahead and walk, Regina," said Dad. "The weather's nice."

Of course the weather was nice. It was her birthday month. Regina looked doubtfully at her paper bag. She couldn't hurt her masterpiece. Her whole future depended on it.

"Out, Regina," said Lydia. "If Maureen doesn't start driving faster than two-miles-per-hour we'll be late, and I wanted to meet Samantha before the bell rings."

"Maureen's doing fine," said Dad.

Regina got out and hitched her backpack over her shoulders, then carefully picked up her bag. Lydia slammed the door. The Rust Bucket shot, then crept away from the curb.

Regina marched toward school, holding her bag before her like one of the Three Wise Men bearing a gift. Just wait until lunch! Liz Glendenning may be cool and exciting all right, but did she have *this?* Regina grinned at her bag. All she had to do was to give it to Matthew.

Of course, Regina wasn't giving it to Matthew because she liked him. She hated him! More than Arley! But with his big mouth, Matthew was the perfect recipient. He'd make such a ruckus after opening the bag the whole class would laugh. Then Margaret could never forget her!

Regina laughed out loud.

A long, older car pulled up to the sidewalk. Kate jumped out. A white-haired lady waved from inside.

"What's so funny?" Kate asked Regina.

Regina tucked her bag under her elbow and straightened guiltily. "Where's your mom?"

Kate snorted. "Don't ask me."

"She is coming today, isn't she?"

Kate glared at Regina. "Can't people talk about something else?"

Fine! If it were up to Regina, she'd never mention Liz Glendenning again. They walked along in silence.

"Oh, there's Margaret," Kate exclaimed when they finally reached the school. She ran forward and whispered something in Margaret's ear. Margaret nodded.

Regina blanketed her tooth with her tongue. Let them have their little secret. Soon Margaret would see who was the most fun friend.

Matthew waved from the doorway of Mr. Amsden's room. "All uglies, step inside!"

"Then you better step back in," called Kate.

Matthew shook his head. "Nope. You first. Stupidity before beauty."

Regina fumed. Matthew should be calling *her* ugly and stupid. Forget about waiting until lunch!

"Guess what I have?" Regina gave her bag an enticing shake.

"Matthew's pacifier," said Kate.

"Kate's underwear," said Matthew.

"Matthew's dandruff," said Kate.

"Kate's drool," said Matthew.

Regina glared at them both. She was supposed

42

to be the one having the fun! "You're wrong. It's something for the boy I love."

"Oh," said Matthew, scratching his arm. "That must be for Robbie."

Regina's mouth fell open. *Robbie?*

Just then Robbie trundled up, his robots tucked against his chest.

"Hey Colberg," said Matthew. "Calhoun has something for you."

Robbie broke into a beatific smile. "She does?"

"Come on, Margaret," said Kate, pulling her into Mr. Amsden's room. "I've got to tell you something."

Regina clamped her hands on her hips as Margaret and Kate walked away. They weren't even watching. Well, she certainly wasn't wasting her creation on Robbie. Her fingers brushed something hard in the pocket of her jumper. The squirt gun.

"Here," she said, tossing it at Robbie.

The squirt gun bounced off the arm in which he cradled his robots. He dropped to the floor to grab it.

"Thanks, Regina!" he said, only a little spit flying.

She ran into the classroom.

"To your desks," said Mr. Amsden. "Bell's going to ring."

Regina slowed down when she saw Margaret and Kate in a huddle. Margaret was forgetting her faster than she thought. She had to get the surprise to Matthew now, but how? She'd never dreamed he wouldn't be interested.

43

"Quickly, quickly," said Mr. Amsden. "We need to get started on Math right after the announcements. Liz Glendenning is coming at ten-thirty."

An excited buzz rippled across the room as kids dropped into their seats. Had it been only yesterday that she'd caused a similiar stir by ordering french fries over the P.A. system? Were those days gone forever?

The announcements came on. Everyone stood for the Lord's Prayer and the Pledge of Allegiance. Then, as kids sat down before Mrs. Yoder took the microphone for the Thought for the Day, Regina saw it: A folded piece of notebook paper slipped forward from Margaret's hand to Kate's.

Regina watched in horrified fascination. Kate opened the note, read it, then laughed. Kate turned around. Her grin froze under Regina's glare.

"Oh, hi, Regina."

"Shhhh!" warned Mr. Amsden.

Regina stared at the back of Margaret's head, willing her to turn around. She had to see Margaret's face. One look in her eyes, and Regina would know if Margaret liked Kate more than her. Margaret's face never lied.

Margaret didn't move, but her ears told Regina all she needed to know. Margaret's ears glowed a fiery red.

Guilty.

Regina felt so weak she could hardly move her tongue to her tooth. She had lost Margaret, *in one day,* and with her birthday coming, too. Regina needed her. She had to get her back—*had*

44

to—but how? How could she prove she was a better best friend than Kate?

Regina drew herself up straighter. The surprise. Proof that she was the most hilarious girl in the fifth grade. Once Regina made a scene with it, Margaret would be proud to be her best friend.

Somehow, she would get the surprise to Matthew. Even if she had to *make* him take it.

8

You Too, Brutus?

Regina hunched in her seat, scowling at the back of Margaret's and Kate's heads as Mr. Amsden explained the finer points of long division on the overhead projector.

"After we get the product of two times one," said Mr. Amsden, "we bring it down under the three. Two is one less than three, so we have a remainder of one."

Regina snorted. Amsden just lost her. Anyway, Regina knew everything there was to know about remainders since Kate had stolen Margaret. Regina was one.

She glanced at the clock. 9:10. In an hour and twenty minutes Mrs. Glendenning would come. Unless Regina wanted to be as forgotten as a drizzly day in March, she had an hour and twenty minutes to get the surprise to Matthew.

Who would have ever figured Matthew'd resist the bait? Just yesterday he would have been the

46

first to snatch out of her hand anything she claimed was for the man she loved. Today he'd practically delivered the bag to Robbie.

Well, she certainly wasn't throwing away her masterpiece on Robbie. No one would even notice that he had it. Who knew how long that booger had hung on his cheek before he'd started chasing Regina, pretending he was a vampire? He could have gone hours with it there.

Mr. Amsden's voice broke through Regina's thoughts. "Regina?"

She jerked upright. "Yes?"

"You snoozing?"

Before Regina could begin to cook up an excuse, Mr. Amsden turned away. "Robbie? How about you giving us the remainder for problem three?"

Robbie hung his head.

Mr. Amsden raised his eyebrows in surprise. "*Et tu,* Robbie?"

"What's *that* supposed to mean?" said Teresa Corvi, scratching her chin with her golden TE-RESA pencil.

"*Et tu?*" Mr. Amsden rolled the marker for the overhead projector between his hands, making it click against his ring. "Back in ancient Roman times, that's what Julius Caesar was supposed to have said when his friends betrayed him."

Regina snapped to attention. *Betrayed by friends?*

"A group of them decided they wanted to rule Rome instead of Caesar," Mr. Amsden continued, clicking away, "so they coaxed him into meeting with them. When they got him alone, they jumped him and all took turns stabbing him."

"Cool!" said Matthew.

Mr. Amsden shook his head. "Not cool. Anyway, when Caesar's best friend, Brutus, made the last stab, Caesar cried, *'Et tu, Brute?'* That means 'You too, Brutus?' in Latin. Shakespeare wrote a play about it."

"And I thought Caesar was a salad!" Matthew declared.

Regina didn't laugh with the rest of the class. Caesar's betrayal sounded too much like her own. Blood rushed to her cheeks. What if Margaret and Kate were thinking the same thing? What a good chuckle they must be having!

Regina stewed in her own embarrassment until Mr. Amsden turned off the overhead projector a few minutes later. "Now that everyone knows what to do with remainders," he said, "page one fifty-one, evens, for homework shouldn't be too tough. Let's try to get in some English before our visitor arrives."

As everyone closed their math books, Regina opened hers. She squinted at page 151. She didn't know how to do that stuff. She'd have to get Margaret to show—

Fear swept over her in a prickly wave. She couldn't ask Margaret. Margaret was Kate's friend now. Regina had nobody.

She laid her head on her arms.

"Regina?" asked Mr. Amsden. "You okay?"

Regina nodded, her bird's nest brushing against her arm.

"Better sit up. You'll want to look alive when our celebrity guest comes."

Regina swallowed back the lump in her throat. *Et tu,* Mr. Amsden?

Mr. Amsden launched into a lesson about pronouns, but Regina didn't hear. She was remembering the last time she had felt this alone.

She had been three. She was walking with her mother and sisters in a Christmastime crowd at the mall when they passed a store window full of stuffed animals. Mom, Maureen, and Lydia plowed forward into the crush of the Food Court; Regina veered off towards the toys.

Regina was hugging a soft raccoon in one arm and a pig that oinked in the other when a white-haired lady with a face as withered as an old apple took her by the hand. "Where's your mommy, dear?"

Only when Regina saw the pitying look in the old lady's puckered face, did she realize something was wrong. Her mother was gone. Maybe forever. Regina had thrown back her head and howled. The howl was still echoing in her ears when Mr. Amsden closed his English book. "Our visitor should be here within the next five or ten minutes. Let's clean up our desks and make her think we look civilized."

Regina glanced at the clock. 10:25, and she still had the bag.

Mr. Amsden retrieved a worn copy of *The Little House on the Prairie* from under a pile of papers on his desk. "How about everyone cleaning up quietly while I read?" He thumbed through the yellowed pages. "Let's see, we were on chapter—"

"Read us that Caesar story!" Matthew exclaimed. "We want to hear the part about the stabbing."

Regina slid low in her chair. They might as well talk about her.

"Regina," Kate whispered, pointing under Regina's desk. "Your underwear!"

Regina bolted upright. There'd be another stabbing scene for that Shakespeare to write about if Kate didn't shut up. She glanced at the crucifix. Okay, she wouldn't stab Kate, but she didn't have to like her.

Two chapters later, Mr. Amsden closed *The Little House on the Prairie*. He looked at the clock. So did Regina. 11:13.

"Why don't we all stand up and stretch a minute?" said Mr. Amsden.

Everyone leaped to their feet . . . except Regina. She laid her head on her desk and closed her eyes. She pictured herself wrapped in a toga, lying dead on the floor, while Kate and Margaret stood over her, shaking hands.

"Regina, what's wrong?"

Regina opened her eyes. Margaret bent over her, a troubled expression behind her round glasses.

"You should know," Regina said testily.

Margaret looked puzzled. "I should?"

"Yes."

Margaret twisted her ponytail. "Give me a hint."

Kate pulled at Margaret's arm. "I told you so! I knew she'd do that."

Regina sat up. "See, there she goes."

Kate sniffed. "Margaret, I need to talk to you. Now."

"Butting in *again!*" Regina exclaimed. "I try to be nice, let her be one of the Awesome Threesome—"

Kate let out a hiccup then rushed, sobbing, into Margaret's arms.

Regina let out a shriek of indignation. She should be the one crying, not Kate.

"Regina," said Margaret, patting Kate's back, "I think you've got the wrong idea. This has nothing to do with you."

"Nothing to do with me?" Regina exclaimed. What about the note? What about the whispering? What about Froot Loops?

But Margaret had quit listening. In Kate's ear, she was whispering, "Shhh, don't cry. She didn't mean anything by this. She loves you, I know she does."

Regina jumped out of her seat. She did not love Kate! She stomped toward Kate to tell her how very much she did *not* love her.

Mr. Amsden stepped between them. "Kate, are you all right?"

Regina gaped in outrage. Why wasn't anyone asking if *she* were all right? She was the one who had lost her best friend! And only three days before her birthday, too!

"Hey Calhoun," Matthew called, leaning against his desk, "if you didn't get Colberg a robot, what did you get him, a box of Kleenex?" He pretended to wipe something from his cheek.

Regina was about to yell, *Shut up, Stink Breath,* when an idea struck her as swiftly as Brutus's knife.

She whipped the paper bag out of her desk and shook it in front of Matthew's face. "My surprise isn't for the boy I love. I gave him something already. *This* surprise is for the boy with the stinkiest breath in the school!"

Instead of snatching at the bag, Matthew stepped backward. He turned his head to give a quick breath into his hand, then frowned.

"Very funny," he muttered before stalking away.

Regina gaped at Matthew, then at her bag. What had gone wrong?

Just then, Mrs. Greenway poked her head inside the classroom. "Mr. Amsden? I've got a message for you."

9

R-ouch!

At the rear of the line meandering its way to the lunchroom, Regina took a long, sad look into her paper bag. How did unloading a surprise on Matthew ever get so hard? Why couldn't he just take it, open it, and scream like usual? Since when had Matthew Rogers become self-conscious about his breath?

Since Margaret had dropped Regina. Since the whole world had gone bad.

Regina refolded the top of the bag, making it even more wrinkled from handling. Well, at least if she wanted to get her surprise off before Mrs. Glendenning came, she had time. According to the secretary, Mrs. Greenway, Liz had gotten tied up with the plane crash story, but was still coming. How late, the secretary didn't know.

The line stopped in front of the restrooms. "Anyone need to use the facilities?" Mr. Amsden asked.

Though Regina didn't have to go, she rushed for the swinging door. Teresa Corvi and a few other girls followed.

Inside the restroom, Regina ran to the farthest stall. She locked the door, and listening as the other girls found their own stalls, perched on the edge of the toilet seat. She opened the brown bag and pulled out the surprise.

A sad smile crept across her face as she turned it in her hands. What a shame it would be to waste this beauty. It was her best invention yet. And making it had been so easy.

Yesterday, when Dad and Lydia had been at Drug World, and Maureen had been in the family room watching Liz on TV, Regina had sneaked open the cupboard above the refrigerator. The Twinkies were waiting for her.

Carefully, so carefully, she removed the plastic wrap around a single spongy loaf. She rooted through the silverware drawer until she found an infant spoon from her own babyhood, then proceeded to drill into the end of the Twinkie.

She scooped out all the filling, only ripping the Twinkie a little. Bones circled her knees like a hungry shark. When she got down the Dog E Dine, he broke into a prance.

Spoonful after tiny spoonful, Bones bouncing at her legs, Regina stuffed the Twinkie. It reminded her of feeding a baby. By the time she'd been done, she'd almost expected the Twinkie to burp.

Now a sniffing sound came from the restroom stall next to Regina's.

"Eeuuww," said Teresa. "What stinks?"

"Nothing!" Regina stowed the Twinkie back into the paper bag.

"Regina, is that you?" Teresa sniffed some more. "I smell dog breath."

Politely, Regina asked, "Have you tried any mouthwash lately?" But Teresa was right. The smell of her surprise was even worse than she remembered. The odor made her so queasy she didn't mind, for the moment, that in her excitement about bringing the Twinkie to school, she'd forgotten her lunch.

She washed her hands and hurried out to the line in the hall, automatically taking her place behind Margaret and Kate. She gasped, realizing she no longer belonged there. Burning with embarrassment, she looked for an escape, but it was too late.

"Troops, ho!" Mr. Amsden said, pointing the way forward. "Let's get lunch finished as fast as we can in case Mrs. Glendenning comes."

"This is so embarrassing," Regina heard Kate whisper to Margaret. "All the other parents are coming next week but *she* had to come today. Now she's late. She doesn't care how stupid she makes me look."

"She does, too," said Margaret.

"Prove it!" said Kate.

Margaret twisted her ponytail. "She wanted to come here, didn't she?"

"Only to show off," said Kate.

"You know that's not true. Anyhow, aren't you proud of her?"

Regina gagged loudly. She couldn't listen anymore. This was more sickening than her Twinkie.

"Regina," came a shy voice behind her. "Are you all right?"

Regina whirled around.

Robbie Colberg cringed. "You—you made that sound. I thought you were going to throw up."

Regina snorted. That was for Matthew to do, or better yet, now that she thought about it, Kate. "I'm okay," she muttered, turning back around. She retuned her ears to Margaret and Kate's conversation.

"Um, Regina?" Robbie whispered.

Regina didn't bother to look at him. "What?"

"About what you asked me yesterday . . ."

"What'd I ask you?"

Robbie cleared his throat, then raised his voice. "If I wanted to go out with—" he ducked his head "—you."

Margaret and Kate turned around. Further ahead, Matthew pulled out of line to stare.

Finally, they noticed her! Regina flashed a triumphant look at Kate. "Yes, Robbie?"

"Well . . ." Robbie gulped. ". . . I do. Want to go with you."

"Great!" said Regina.

Margaret sighed. "Oh, Regina."

Regina clutched Robbie's arm in defiance. Margaret didn't care about her anymore. What gave her the right to disapprove?

"Well," said Kate, "I guess that makes you Mr. and Mrs. Mad Dog, doesn't it? Now I was saying, Margaret—"

"That's right!" Regina let go of Robbie to spring at Kate. "I am Mrs. Mad Dog. Let's get her, Mr. Mad Dog!" Regina snapped her jaws, pretending to attack. "Ruff! Ruff!"

An astonished smile crossed Robbie's face. He blundered forward. "Ruff! Ruff Ruff!" Spit flew as he barked. Kate drew back in disgust.

Laughing, Regina bounded toward Matthew. She grabbed his arm and opened her mouth wide for a huge pretend bite.

"Regina!" Mr. Amsden shouted. "That's enough. Take your lunch and get back to the room—now! If you can't act like a human being, you can eat alone."

"Ruff!" Robbie barked. "Rat's ry rife!"

"What?" exclaimed Mr. Amsden.

Matthew squinted. "I think he said, 'That's my wife.'"

"Oh." Mr. Amsden frowned. "Well, far be it from me to separate married couples. Colberg, you're lunching in the room, too."

Robbie grinned. "Ro-kay!"

"Eating in the room is not supposed to be a picnic, Robbie," Mr. Amsden said. "You two just earned yourselves a detention."

Robbie sucked in his breath. It was his first detention ever. He glanced at Regina, then wiped at his eye.

Regina touched her tongue to her tooth. After a long moment, she pulled on his bony arm. "Come on, Mr. Mad Dog. You get used to 'em after a while."

Robbie followed, sniffing.

Regina sighed as she trudged toward the room. Robbie had nothing to cry about. He'd only lost a perfect behavior record. Regina hadn't had one since preschool.

She, on the other hand, had lost something far more serious. She had just lost her chance to get back her best friend forever. She would be turning eleven alone. No party, no presents, no Margaret.

10

Newlyweds

Regina leaned against the back of her chair, frowning at the now very wrinkled bag on her desk. In his desk, two rows over, Robbie Colberg crunched on a hard granola bar.

Regina sighed. "Do you think you could eat that thing a little less loudly?"

Robbie stopped in the middle of chewing. He choked down an entire mouthful. "Yes, dear."

"That's another thing. You've called me 'dear' three times since we got back to the room. You have to stop that."

Robbie hung his head, his scalp scarlet through his wispy dark hair. "That's what my parents call each other. I thought since we were married . . ." He trailed off, hanging his head lower.

Regina glanced at the crucifix, then groaned. "Okay, okay. Just don't expect me to call you 'dear' back."

"All right—" Robbie peeked at Regina "—dear."

Regina stifled a moan. If she had to have only one admirer left in the world, at least he was a sincere one.

Robbie returned to gnawing at his granola bar. Regina had hunkered down in her seat and was poking at her bag when a flash of gold on the floor caught her eye. One of Teresa's TERESA pencils had rolled into the aisle by Regina's desk.

Regina raised her eyebrows. Teresa never let her possessions out of her sight. No one was allowed to touch anything that had a golden TERESA on it. Teresa said her father would come after anyone who did.

Regina gazed at the pencil, then leaned over and scooped it up. She frowned at the shining TERESA, then covered the TE and SA with her fingers. The R and the remaining E looked almost like her own initials.

"Why aren't you eating your lunch?" Robbie asked.

Regina thrust the pencil in her desk. "What?"

"You've just been playing with your bag. Why don't you eat your food? You'll get hungry . . . dear." He smiled sheepishly.

Regina looked at the sack containing her surprise. No excuse would come to mind.

Robbie reached into his Robot Man lunchbox, opened a plastic container, and held it out over the neighboring desk. "Want some grapes?"

Regina put her hand over her stomach. It was achingly empty. She reached over the desk between them. "Thanks," she said, breaking off a grape.

"Take the whole container." Robbie gave her the grapes. "I've got some peanut butter and crackers you can have, too," he said, digging in his lunchbox.

Regina took the Baggie full of saltine crackers smeared with peanut butter. They were just like the ones she made at home.

"I eat them all the time," Robbie explained. "They're my favorite snack."

Regina took a bite. Who would have thought she had something in common with Robbie Colberg?

They munched in comfortable silence. When Robbie finished, he got out his robots, and began staging a war on his desk.

"Zap! Zap Zap!"

Regina wiped the cracker crumbs from her face with the back of her hand. "Um, Robbie?"

"Zap Zap! Yes, dear?"

"Do you have to play with robots?"

Robbie's brow buckled. "Don't you like them?"

"Sure I like them . . . but . . . maybe other people don't."

Robbie looked confused. "Why wouldn't they like them?"

"I don't know. Maybe they think they're weird."

Robbie jerked back as if hit. "Weird?" He slumped in his chair. "I never thought about that."

He stared mournfully at his robots. When he looked up, his eyes were so full of trust it made something hurt in Regina's chest. "Do you think I should get rid of them?"

Regina sat with her tongue against her tooth. After a long, silent moment, she sighed. "What are their names?"

Robbie blinked. "My robots? You really want to know?"

Regina nodded.

Robbie straightened, then held up each robot in turn, a grin widening across his thin face. "Lazar. Zakar. Mole—he's the bad one. Vott—he used to be bad, but now he's good. Nadar—"

He was interrupted by the pounding of size ten-and-a-half adult sneakers. "Oh, look," said Matthew, jogging into the room, "if it isn't the newlyweds."

Robbie beamed. Regina slid under her desk.

Kate pointed as she walked with Margaret to Regina's desk. "Underwear."

Regina wound up to explode, but was cut short by a shriek two seats ahead.

"My pencil is missing!" Teresa exclaimed. "I left it on my desk when I went to lunch and now it's gone!"

"Have you tried looking in your desk?" said Mr. Amsden, turning on the lights as he walked into the room.

Teresa bobbed her head toward the opening of her desk. "There's only five! I had six!"

Regina's hand crept toward the TERESA pencil in her desk. She had forgotten she'd put it in there. Well, no use in making a scene. When school was over, she'd just slip it back in Teresa's—

Kate pointed to Regina's desk. "There's your pencil, Teresa."

Regina's cheeks blazed. "How'd it get in there?" She glanced at Margaret. Disappointment was written all over Margaret's face.

"Is my dad going to be mad at you!" Teresa exclaimed. "Don't be surprised when he calls you tonight, Regina Calhoun."

Sweat trickled down Regina's face and back. She felt as if she were melting from her own heat. "I was giving it back. I didn't mean—"

Robbie didn't let her finish. "Teresa," he cried, spit flying, "why don't you just tell your dad the Pet Man to go brush himself!"

Teresa's mouth fell open. So did Regina's.

Mr. Amsden passed his ring hand over his mouth as if wiping away a smile. "That's enough, Robbie. Regina, give Teresa her pencil. Teresa, just let this one go, okay? Now everyone get situated so we can begin our science lesson."

Kate trotted to her desk. Margaret took her seat, but not before giving Regina one last disapproving frown.

Regina ran her hand through her bird's nest. Now she'd really ruined it with Margaret. Who'd want to be friends with a person married to Mad Dog Colberg when they could be friends with Liz Glendenning's daughter? Especially when Mad Dog's wife looked like a thief.

Now she not only looked bad to Margaret, but to the whole class. Unless she counted Robbie. And what was she going to do with him?

11

It's Me, Dear

"Sit, Bones, sit."

Regina held an opened can of Dog E Dine over Bones's head. He wiggled into an anxious sit.

"Good boy." She banged the loaf from the can into Bones's bowl. Though it was his third can that sunny Saturday morning, he attacked it as if he hadn't eaten in weeks. Bones clearly preferred canned dog food to dry. Regina didn't know why her parents made him eat the dry chow. She didn't.

"Glad to see you're taking such good care of Bones," said Mom, padding into the kitchen in her slippers. "Dad told me he had put you in charge of him."

"It's easy," said Regina, resting her elbows on the counter to watch her mother wash out the coffeepot. She sighed elaborately. "I wish everything were that easy."

Mom looked over, steam rising from the sink where she worked. "Do you have a problem, Regina?"

Regina sucked in her breath. "Yes," she said as Bones sunk down by her feet and laid his head on his paws.

"Tell me."

That was all the invitation Regina needed. She told her mother how Kate had stolen away Margaret, how Margaret had not minded being stolen, how Margaret had *stayed* stolen even though Mrs. Glendenning had never made it to school yesterday. In fact, Regina exclaimed, Mrs. Glendenning's absence seemed to make Margaret pay more attention to Kate than ever.

"She doesn't even like me anymore," Regina said, her voice breaking.

Mom turned on the coffeemaker. "You finished?"

Regina nodded. Somehow, she just didn't feel like talking about becoming Mrs. Mad Dog.

"Regina," said Mom, wiping her hands on a dishtowel, "people don't steal people. If someone wants to be friends with you, they will. Other people can't force them away."

"You don't know Kate," Regina muttered, rocking Bones's body with her toe.

"I do know Margaret." Mom put two slices of bread in the toaster. "Are you sure she doesn't want to be friends anymore? That doesn't sound like her."

"Positive!"

"Why would you think that?"

"She's always talking to Kate. All Kate has to

do is pretend like she's crying, and Margaret comes running."

"Kate cries?"

Regina moved her toe to rub Bones's ribs. He closed his eyes in ecstasy. "Oh, Kate just acts like she's crying to get attention. She has nothing to cry about. She's the one with the famous exciting cool mom."

"Not to be confused with us unknown boring tacky moms," said Mom, getting the butter dish from the refrigerator.

"I didn't mean—"

"I'm kidding, Regina. I'm fine with who I am." She put the butter on the counter. "You said Liz Glendenning didn't make it to school yesterday, and everyone was expecting her. Don't you think that was hard on Kate?"

Regina tossed her hands. "No one held it against her if her mom didn't come! Mrs. Glendenning's famous. She can do what she wants."

The toast popped up. Bones skittered to his feet and trotted over to Mom as she put the toast on a plate and started buttering it. "Maybe Kate doesn't see it that way, Regina. Maybe Kate takes it as a sign that she's not important to her mother."

"Oh, that's not true! Any dummy can tell that her mother's crazy over her. She gives Kate whatever she wants."

"People don't always see what may seem obvious to others." Mom finished buttering the toast and offered Regina a slice. Bones peered intently at the plate, wagging his tail.

"No, Bones," said Mom, "none for you." She cocked her head, frowning. "Am I mistaken, or has he gained weight? Regina, how much have you been—"

The phone rang.

"Grab it," said Mom, "before it wakes up Maureen and Lydia."

Regina scampered to the wall phone over the counter, her heart pounding. Let it be Margaret!

"Hello?"

"Regina?"

Regina puzzled over the unfamiliar male voice. "Who is this?"

"It's me . . . *dear*."

Regina closed her eyes, then covered the receiver. "It's for me, Mom."

Mom nodded, then stepped outside to get the newspaper.

Regina waited until Mom was out of earshot. "What do you want, Robbie?"

"I'm sorry to call you so early, dear—but I couldn't wait! You know how you gave me a present?"

Regina thought of the miniature squirt gun. She remembered how disappointed she'd been when she'd pulled it out of the cereal box. What a rip-off! It made her feel like not eating any Nutty Nuggets for a while.

"Well," said Robbie, "I've got one for you, too."

"Me?" She frowned. "A little squirt gun?"

"Oh, no! I got you something else." Robbie's voice was filled with distress. "Did you want a squirt gun?"

"No, that's okay," said Regina, perking up. Getting a present from Robbie was better than getting a present from nobody. After all, her birthday was the day after tomorrow. "What did you get me?"

"My mom picked it out."

"Oh."

"It was real expensive."

"Oh!"

"You'll be getting it at—" Robbie broke off, giggling. "I almost told the surprise!"

"What surprise?"

"Can't tell."

"Tell me!"

"Can't."

A new thought worried Regina. She waited as Mom returned inside the kitchen with the newspaper, poured herself a cup of coffee, then strolled into the family room.

"How expensive is expensive?" Regina whispered into the phone.

Robbie chuckled. "*Real* expensive."

"Like ten dollars?"

"All I know is I told my mom you loved me, then she came home with *this*."

Regina gulped. "She thinks I love you?"

"She doesn't think it, she knows it!"

"Robbie, I have to go. I need to—" She noticed Bones still waiting at her feet "—feed the dog." In order to make it not a lie, the moment she hung up, she gave Bones another can of dog food.

Dad strolled into the kitchen in his robe, his bird's nest crushed to one side. "Morning, Regina.

I see you're keeping up with your dog care duties. Way to go."

"Thanks." Regina waited until Dad poured himself some coffee and joined Mom in the family room. She pounded numbers into the phone.

With Bones waiting patiently at her feet, Regina held her breath and listened as the phone rang. This could be the dumbest call she'd ever made.

12

The Odor

Hang up right now, Regina told herself as the phone rang on. *Hang up before you get your feelings more hurt. Hang up before—*

She heard Margaret's voice on the other end of the line. "Hello?"

Regina gave Bones a nervous pat. "Margaret, you awake?"

"Regina, where were you last night? I tried calling and calling and no one would answer."

"You did?" After school yesterday, Regina had taken the phone off the hook until Maureen and Lydia came home later that evening from a soccer game and put it back on. Regina had been afraid Dr. Corvi would call, angry about Teresa's pencil. She also couldn't bear listening for phone calls from Margaret she was sure would never come. "You really called?"

"Of course I did. You know we always do something together Friday night."

"Aren't you mad that I stole Teresa's pencil?"

"Did you steal it?"

"No."

"I didn't think you would."

Regina caught her breath. "I thought you were mad," she said, remembering Margaret's disapproving look.

"About the pencil? Of course I wasn't. Everyone knows how Teresa blows things out of proportion."

Regina did a little dance, making Bones prance at her feet. Mom was right. Kate hadn't stolen Margaret away. Margaret still liked her!

"So what's up?" Margaret asked.

Regina straightened, remembering what had made her brave the call. "Margaret, I have a bad problem."

"Yes?" Margaret's voice was full of worry.

Already Regina felt a million times better. Telling Margaret her problems was like performing a worry transplant. How could Regina have survived without her?

"Margaret, Robbie's getting me an expensive present."

"How do you know?"

"He told me just now on the phone."

"Oh, Regina."

Regina detected disappointment in Margaret's voice. "Don't worry, I've been nice to him!"

To Regina's surprise, Margaret gasped. "Oh no. Did he say why he was giving it to you?"

Wasn't that obvious? "Because he loves me."

"Oh! I was afraid it was something else." Margaret sounded relieved.

71

Regina frowned. "Don't you get it? He gave me something expensive. That's bad, because I don't really love him."

"Oh, Regina. Why did you pretend—"

Just then, the phone clicked on Margaret's end of the line. "Regina, what do you think about Arley's present?"

Regina's heart froze. "Kate?" Bones nudged her on the leg with his cold nose, causing her to shiver.

"I'm in Margaret's room," said Kate. "She's in the kitchen. So don't you think Arley's present to Margaret was cute?"

"I haven't told Regina yet," Margaret said.

Regina sagged. Mom was wrong. Kate *had* taken her place.

"You didn't?" said Kate. "Oh, Margaret, how could you not tell her? It is so cute! Regina, Arley gave Kate this little bitty squirt gun. It's adorable. He said he's got one, too. They're going to squirt each other in class."

"It's just a little bit of water," Margaret explained.

"Margaret and I tried it on each other last night," Kate said, laughing. "You should have seen us! At first we hardly got wet, then Margaret snuck out and got an empty dish soap bottle from her mother."

Margaret chuckled on her end of the line.

"She really blasted me!" Kate cried. "Of course I had to whomp her one with a wet washcloth. From then on, it was war! Boy, did we get the bathroom sopping! Water was all over the mirror."

Margaret chortled. "You would have loved it, Regina!"

Regina could hardly breathe. "I know where Arley got that squirt gun! From a cereal box. I got one, too. It was so cheap I gave it to Robbie!"

A strained silence hummed over the phone line. Bones peered into Regina's face, then nuzzled his nose into her hand to lick her palm.

Kate's icy voice filled the phone. "We have to go, Regina. We're going to go play with Margaret's cheap squirt gun." There was a loud click.

So softly that Regina could barely hear her, Margaret said, "Oh, Regina, can't you ever be happy for someone?" A slow click followed.

Regina held the receiver, scarcely feeling Bones licking her free hand, until the operator came on. "If you'd like to make a call—"

Regina hung up. She'd blown it. Forever.

Maureen dragged into the room, her hands rolled into her droopy T-shirt, exposing the top of her boxers. "Oh," she groaned, "why does lifeguard certification class have to be so early in the morning?"

Regina cast a miserable gaze in her direction.

Half of Maureen's mouth edged up in a sleepy smile. "Now there's someone who looks worse than I do. What's wrong, Goof?"

Regina sighed long and hard. "Everyone hates me."

"Though I could see why they would," said Maureen, opening the refrigerator, which auto-

73

matically made Bones leave Regina to take his post by the meat drawer, "I doubt that's true."

"It is true. Even Margaret does."

"I can't believe sweet little Margaret would ever hate anyone."

"You don't understand. I *made* her hate me!"

"Well, now that I can imagine." Maureen pushed aside the orange juice container to pull out the milk.

"It's not funny!" Regina cried. "And I'm in trouble, too."

Maureen got a bowl out of the cupboard, Bones following. "So what's new?"

"You'll stop laughing when Dr. Corvi calls the police on me!"

Maureen set her bowl on the counter and stared at Regina. "What'd you do?"

"I accidentally stole Teresa's pencil."

Maureen crossed her arms over her T-shirt. "Oh, now that's criminal. You can get the electric chair for that."

"He *is* mad!" Regina exclaimed. "And that's not even my worst problem."

Maureen got out two biscuits of Shredded Wheat, and under Bones's watchful eye, broke them up in her bowl.

When Maureen didn't respond, Regina cried, "Don't you care that some boy is giving me a very expensive present his mother picked out, and I don't even like him? He thinks we're married!"

Maureen burst out laughing.

"It's serious! What if his mom comes after me and makes me marry him when we get older?"

"Oh, Regina." Maureen stopped laughing and made a terrible face. "Oh, Bones!"

A sharp, sickening odor burned Regina's nose. Bones sunk to his belly, a pained doggy smile on his face.

"That's hideous!" Maureen waved her hands. "Bones, what have you been eating?

Dad strolled in the kitchen with his coffee cup. "Whew! What died?"

"He stinks!" Maureen gasped, pointing at Bones as she waved. "I think he's sick!"

Dad held his nose and peered at Bones, who had rolled over on his side. "You know, he does look bloated."

Regina stared at Bones's belly, dread descending upon her like a cold, wet blanket.

"Regina," asked Dad, "what have you been feeding him?"

Regina gulped. "Just his food."

Dad opened the cupboard where the dog food was kept. "Where'd all the cans go? I bought fifteen of them on sale a couple days ago. Now they're gone."

Regina clamped her tongue to her tooth. "He wanted them." It was the truth.

"He wanted them *all?* In two days?"

"I told you she couldn't handle it!" said Maureen. "He's probably going to explode!"

Bones wasn't going to explode, was he? Tears burned Regina's eyes as she pictured bits of yellow dog all over the kitchen. "You said I'd forget to feed him," she said, holding back a sob.

"So you went crazy in the opposite direction!"

Maureen cried. "Regina, why do you always have to overdo things? Why can't you ever be good?"

"That's enough, Maureen." Dad knelt by Bones's side. "I'll take over Bones now," he said, tenderly patting the dog's extended stomach. Regina slunk out of the room.

Why *couldn't* she be good?

13

The Goodest of Good

Monday, Regina shuffled at the end of the line as her class made its way to the lunchroom. She rolled and unrolled the wrinkled bag in her hand, her heart aching with loneliness. Who would have ever thought her eleventh birthday would be so miserable?

Mr. Amsden stopped the group in front of the restrooms. "Whoever needs to use the facilities, you know who you are."

Several kids broke out of line, including Margaret and Kate. Regina watched as they ran, chattering, into the bathroom. Margaret hadn't talked to her all morning.

Robbie crept behind Regina and cleared his throat. "Will you sit with me at lunch, dear?"

"Can't." Regina glanced at the wrinkled bag in her hands. "There's something I need to do."

It was true. Saturday, when Bones's gut had become as overextended as a filled water balloon,

Regina promised God that if he kept Bones from exploding, she would try to become good. That meant apologizing to Robbie for pretending to love him. Promising Teresa she'd never touch another of her things. Confessing to Margaret about her selfish plan to steal Margaret's attention when Mrs. Glendenning came. That included being nice to Kate, even on Regina's own birthday. She'd be the *goodest* of good.

Bones had lived.

Now Robbie sighed with disappointment. "Well, at least I get to be with you after school."

"After school?" Regina bit her lip in alarm. Was Robbie's mother waiting for her after school with the gift? How was she going to tell Robbie she didn't love him without infuriating Mrs. Colberg? Being good was scarier than she thought.

Robbie slapped his forehead and groaned. "I wasn't supposed to tell!"

"Don't tell!" Regina cried. "Don't even give it to me! I don't deserve it."

"Don't deserve what?" asked Robbie.

They stared at each other in confusion.

"Aren't you talking about my present?" Regina asked.

Mr. Amsden held a stubby finger to his lips just as Robbie opened his mouth to answer. "Quiet in line!" Mr. Amsden ordered.

Margaret and Kate scuttled out of the restroom. Neither bothered to look at Regina.

Robbie watched them, frowning. "They are still having it, aren't they?" he whispered.

"Still having what?"

"Regina!" Mr. Amsden warned. "Everyone—I want total silence for the rest of the way to the cafeteria. You've all been chattering like a bunch of monkeys."

Before Saturday, those words would have been an open invitation for Regina to break into a hilarious chimpanzee act. Today, even though it was her birthday, she resisted the urge. Maureen was wrong, Regina thought, standing perfectly still. She *was* good. So good Margaret would *have* to take her back.

When the class reached the cafeteria, Regina hustled to where Margaret and Kate sat. She knew which table. A few days ago, it had been hers.

"Hello, Regina," Kate said, looking up nonchalantly. "You going to be nice to Margaret today?"

"Kate," Margaret murmured, blushing. "Happy birthday, Regina."

Regina's words came out in a rush. "Oh, Margaret, I'm so sorry! I should have never said that about Arley's squirt gun. I'm really glad that he likes you, I really am. I don't know what got into me—I was crazy! But I'm different now, you'll see. I'm going to be the kindest, most thoughtful, best person around."

"Good luck," said Kate.

"Oh, Regina," said Margaret, "I shouldn't have taken it so hard about the squirt gun."

Regina shook her head so hard her bird's nest bobbed. "No, Margaret, I was the wrong one! I can see that now because I've changed. From now on, everyone else's feelings come first. See this?"

Regina held up the bag with the dogfood-filled Twinkie inside.

"Is that your lunch?" asked Kate.

"Oh, no." Regina smiled sadly. "You wouldn't believe what I was going to do last week when your mother came."

"I'd believe anything." Kate squashed her sandwich under her fist, then gave the flattened remains a black look. "I hope you weren't counting on her. I never do."

"Oh, I was," said Regina, not noticing Margaret putting her finger to her lips in warning. "I was going to—"

Shoes thundering, Matthew streaked past and snatched the bag out of Regina's hands. "This for me?"

Regina jumped from her seat, her heart leaping into her throat. "Give that back!"

Jogging backward, Matthew opened the bag and looked inside. "Um, yum, a Twinkie!" He grinned at Regina. "On me, they have the effect of breath mints."

"It's not for you!"

Matthew stopped, his big shoulders drooping. "You really do like Colberg, don't you?" He plodded to the next table over, where Robbie sat alone. "Here," said Matthew, tossing the bag in front of Robbie. "It's from your wife."

Robbie looked at Regina, a questioning smile twitching on his face. He opened the bag.

"NO!" screamed Regina.

Robbie jolted upright, blinking.

She raced to Robbie's table and whipped the bag from his hands. "Sorry, I need this!"

Robbie gaped at his empty hands. He looked up, crushed.

Regina bit her lip. This was going all wrong. "Look, Robbie, I'll make it up to you."

Matthew guffawed loudly. "Everyone hear that? Regina said she was going to make out with Colberg! Whoa, Regina, when are you going to kiss him, at the party?"

"The party?" Regina turned just in time to see Margaret and Kate scissoring their arms behind her back.

"What party?" Regina asked, her voice quavering.

Kate shot Matthew a poisoned look. "What are you talking about? There's no party, Regina."

Matthew ducked his head, his face a violent shade of red. "I guess I was thinking of something else."

The roar of cafeteria flooded Regina's ears. The floor seemed to rise beneath her feet. They were having a party without her!

Kate glanced at Margaret, then cleared her throat. "So, Regina, who's the Twinkie for?"

The roaring in Regina's head raised to a deafening howl. Forget being good, forget Margaret, forget everything! "The Twinkie's for you!"

14

Destroying the Evidence

Kate pointed to herself, a confused expression on her face. "For me? Really?" She glanced at Margaret.

Regina glared at her bag. She'd seen the way Kate looked at Margaret. Kate deserved a dogfood-filled Twinkie. "Yes."

Margaret raised her brows.

Kate managed an uncomfortable smile. "Regina, you *are* being nice."

Regina's stomach hardened into a painful knot. How much better she'd felt when she was trying to be good! But they wouldn't let her; *Kate* wouldn't let her.

Kate stood up. "I wasn't going to eat, but now I guess I will. I'm going to go buy a milk."

Margaret leaned toward Regina as Kate strode to the lunch counter. "Regina," she said in a confidential whisper, "thanks for being so nice to Kate. She's been so upset about her mother lately."

"Why would she be upset about her mother?" Regina said, shifting uneasily. Mom had been wrong about Margaret still wanting to be best friends. She had to be wrong about Kate and her mother, too. "Anyone would die to be Liz Glendenning's daughter."

Margaret shrugged. "I know it's weird, but that's how Kate feels." She smiled. "But I'm proud of you. You really have changed."

Guilt slithered through Regina like a snake. But if Margaret really was her friend, how could she make plans without her?

"What's this about a party?" Regina asked.

Margaret blushed. "Oh. That. It's one of Kate's ideas. I'll tell you about it later. Just promise you'll always be my best friend, okay?"

Regina nodded, sick with guilt. So she had been wrong about Margaret. How could she always be so wrong, and everyone else so right? Even Maureen was right. Regina couldn't be good. If Kate ate the Twinkie, everyone would know just how bad Regina really was.

Kate trotted back to the table and took her seat. "Thanks, Regina. You know, a Twinkie really does sound good right now." She reached for the bag.

Margaret winked at Regina.

The hair on Regina's arms stood up in alarm. She hugged the bag to her chest. "NO!"

Kate frowned. "What?"

Matthew sauntered over. "What's all this yelling about?"

"What I mean is, Kate," Regina said in a rush,

"let me bring you another one. This one's . . . stale!" It was the truth. After sitting in an open wrapper all weekend, the Twinkie had to be as stiff as it was smelly.

"Oh, I don't care," said Kate. "I'm in the mood for something sweet." She waggled her fingers in a give-me gesture at the bag.

Regina hugged the bag closer. "Let me get you something else."

Kate pulled back, narrowing her eyes. "What's the matter, Regina? Is there something wrong with that Twinkie?"

Sweat poured down Regina's face. She had to destroy the evidence. Her gaze sidled to the trash can.

Kate sniffed. "Wait a minute. I smell something." She sniffed again. "I do. It's . . ."

Kate sprang at Regina. Regina crammed the Twinkie into her mouth.

". . . DOG FOOD!" Matthew cried.

Kate shrunk back. Margaret gasped.

"REGINA CALHOUN EATS DOG FOOD!" Matthew yelled.

Regina sat very still, water pouring from her eyes. The Twinkie rested, whole, in her mouth.

"She's turning purple," said Kate.

"Green!" cried Matthew.

"Swallow it!" Margaret cried. "Oh, no, she's going to—"

Regina jerked to the side. Everyone leaped from their seats.

When she was done ridding herself of the

84

Twinkie and what was left of her breakfast, she leaned, panting, against the table.

Behind Regina, someone yelled, "Look, it's her!"

Regina closed her eyes. It was starting already. She knew how kids who'd thrown up in school were treated. They were pointed at for days. Weeks. Months!

Kate's happy voice rang in Regina's ears. "She's here!"

Regina opened her eyes. In the doorway with her camera crew and Mrs. Yoder, her hand over her mouth, stood Liz Glendenning.

15

∾

Upsey, Daisy

"Oh, my goodness," said Liz Glendenning as everyone in the entire cafeteria gaped at her and her television crew, "it looks like there's been an accident."

"Apparently so," said Mrs. Yoder, the throbbing vein on her neck even visible from where Regina still sagged against the table. Liz Glendenning strode, high heels clicking, to where Kate huddled with Margaret two tables away from Regina. Liz wrapped Kate in her arms. "Are you okay?"

Kate nodded.

Mrs. Yoder came over and touched Liz Glendenning on the arm, then smiled over her shoulder at the camera crew. "Would you like to go back to the office?" she said to Mrs. Glendenning. "I'll be there in a moment."

Liz grinned. "Good idea. It'll give my daughter and I a minute to catch up." She turned Kate toward the door.

Tears welled up in Kate's eyes as she glanced behind at Margaret.

Told you she'd come, Margaret mouthed to Kate, grinning.

Meanwhile, Regina cringed as Mrs. Yoder marched in her direction. "Re-GI-NA!"

Liz Glendenning's voice rang across the cafeteria. "Wait, Kate. Is that Regina? Oh, dear, and we were having a party for her today."

Regina sat up. Party for her?

"I don't think Miss Calhoun will be going to any parties today," Mrs. Yoder declared, coming to a standstill behind Regina. "Upsey daisy, Regina. Let's see if we can make it back to the clinic."

Regina sprang to her feet, but Kate and her mother were already gone.

"My, my," said Mrs. Yoder, talking through her nose—the smell was strong. "What an amazing recovery."

Later, as Regina lay on the cot in the clinic, waiting for her mother to pick her up, Margaret slipped inside the room.

"Regina, are you okay?"

Regina popped up. "Margaret! What's this about a party for me?"

Margaret laughed. "You didn't guess?"

"No!"

"You mean you didn't wonder about Kate passing me notes all the time?"

"Well, no."

"About her and I meeting secretly after school without you?"

"Noooo . . ."

"About Matthew calling Kate?"

"Noooo . . ."

"Matthew never calls Kate. But after she asked him to come, he called back every day wanting to know what to wear, what to bring, how early to come, and so on. He was so excited about the party he about blew the surprise. The boy is crazy about you, Regina."

Regina's tongue found her tooth. For once in her life she was speechless.

"Why else would we act so mysterious around your birthday? You know I never leave you out on purpose."

Regina smiled weakly. Maureen and Kate were right. She did overdo things. Even her imagination went overboard. When would she ever stop?

Margaret sighed with happiness. "There were so many plans to make! Everyone was invited— even Robbie. You should have seen him, Regina. He was so happy when I asked him, he threw his robots in the air."

Regina laughed. Her smile faded. "But one thing. What are Froot Loops?"

Margaret waved her hand. "I was going to surprise you, but since Kate's mom postponed the party for I don't know how long, I guess I can tell you. I got you an Olympic T-shirt for your birthday. Kate teases me by saying the rings on it look like Froot Loops."

Regina lay back, a lump forming in her throat. "I thought you liked Kate better. I thought she stole you away."

Margaret drew back, frowning. "How could she do that? The only person who could come between me and you is you. Because as long as you want me, I'll be your best friend."

Regina swallowed back the burning lump. "That'll be forever."

Mr. Amsden leaned into the room. "How's the patient?"

"Okay." Regina struggled up on an elbow.

"Glad to hear that." Mr. Amsden laughed, then shook his head at Regina. "You. I heard you ate a doctored-up Twinkie. What was in it, anyway?"

Regina blushed. Margaret must not have believed Matthew's accusation, and Mr. Kraus had cleaned up the evidence quickly. Because surely if Margaret knew what Regina almost did to Kate, she wouldn't want to be best friends.

"Let's just say," Margaret said before Regina could answer, "the filling was just right for Mrs. Mad Dog."

Matthew stuck his head inside the door. "Mr. Amsden? Mrs. Glendenning sent me down to say her camera crew is ready to tape the class."

Mr. Amsden straightened. "Great! Come on guys. Get well, Tiger," he called to Regina as he marched away.

Margaret winked, then scampered out.

Matthew fidgeted at the door. "Oh, here!" he muttered, drawing something from his pocket and tossing it at Regina.

Regina caught a tube of breath mints. She looked up.

"I got myself a matching set," Matthew mumbled. "Maybe we can see if they work sometime."

"What's that supposed to mean?" Regina cried.

Matthew darted from the room. "That's for me to know," he called as he ran away, "and for you to find out!"

"I dare you!" Regina screeched after him.

She sunk down on her cot, her heart thudding as loudly as the footsteps retreating down the hall.

With a sigh, she turned on her side and rolled the mints back and forth on her cot. It would have been nice to have been on TV. It would have been nice to have her own surprise party. It would have been nice to try out the breath mints on Matthew right now. But now at least she knew she had the most important thing of all. Margaret's friendship. And, she realized, Kate's. Maybe the three of them could be buddies. After all, it was harder to fall down riding a tricycle than riding a two-wheeler.

A clumsy pattering of feet sounded outside the clinic. Regina sat up as Robbie Colberg ducked inside the room.

"I'm not supposed to be here," he whispered, "but I wanted you to have this." He thrust a thin wrapped package in her lap.

Regina groaned. "Robbie, I can't take this."

He hung his head. "You can't?"

Regina drew in her breath. She may be bad, but let one thing she did turn out good.

"Robbie?"

He kept his face pointed at the ground. "What?"

"You know when I said that I wanted to go out with you?"

"Yes."

"I shouldn't have said that."

A painful silence filled the tiny room.

"But you know what?"

Robbie whispered softly. "What?"

"I'm glad we did go out together."

He looked up. "You are?"

"Yes. You're the best Mad Dog husband a girl could ever have." She laughed. "You were ferocious when Teresa attacked me!"

Robbie snuffled with pleasure. "Ranything ror rou, Rear."

Regina chuckled.

Robbie's smile faded. "So no presents?"

"No presents." Regina held out the thin package.

"Not even a cheap one?" Robbie's face turned pink. "The present I thought my mom got for you turned out to be for my sister's graduation. But Mom took me shopping yesterday and I got you that." He nodded at the package.

"It's cheap?" said Regina, lowering the present. Maybe a cheap present wouldn't hurt. After all, it was her birthday.

"Real cheap."

Regina ripped it open. A pencil with a golden REGINA embossed on its side shone in the clinic light.

"Gotta go!" Robbie fastwalked to the door.

"Hey, Robbie!" Regina called, her face shining brighter than the golden REGINA. "Thank you . . . dear!"

She laid back on the cot, clutching her pencil to her chest. To herself, she whispered, "Rappy Rirthday, Re-rina!"